Cold Whispers

The GHOST at THE GRAND INN

by Michael Teitelbaum

illustrated by Anthony Resto

BEARPORT
PUBLISHING

New York, New York

Credits
Cover, © Pgiam/iStock and © Alina G/Shutterstock.

Publisher: Kenn Goin
Editorial Director: Natalie Lunis
Creative Director: Spencer Brinker
Text produced by Scout Books & Media Inc.

Library of Congress Cataloging-in-Publication Data in process at time
of publication (2016)
Library of Congress Control Number: 2015013372
ISBN-13: 978-1-62724-808-2 (library binding)

For more information, write to Bearport Publishing Company, Inc.,
45 West 21st Street, Suite 3B, New York, New York 10010.
Printed in the United States of America.

10 9 8 7 6 5 4 3 2 1

Contents

CHAPTER 1

Worst Weekend Ever!

Craig and Melanie Hoffman sat in the backseat of their parents' car, just inches away from each other.

Twelve-year-old Craig slid his left hand toward his sister.

"Hey! You're on my side!" cried eleven-year-old Melanie.

"Am not!" Craig shot back.

"Mom!" Melanie whined. "Craig is on my side."

"Am I going to have to listen to you two fight all weekend?" asked Mom.

"Yeah," replied Craig, "since we're going to some dumb old hotel instead of to a water park, like we wanted! I could have gone on a giant water slide. Instead, I'll be stuck at some hotel with *her*."

Craig leaned over toward Melanie and stuck out his tongue.

"The Grand Inn at the Mountaintop is hardly 'some dumb old hotel,'" Dad said. "It's one of the most **historic** inns in the whole country, just filled with amazing stories from the past."

A few hours later, the Hoffmans turned onto a narrow, bumpy dirt road. As they drove around a bend, The Grand Inn at the Mountaintop came into view.

"Oh no," said Melanie. "This is even worse than I thought!"

The inn was covered in peeling paint. Shutters dangled from windows, flapping in the breeze. The front porch **sagged**.

"This is going to be the worst weekend ever," moaned Craig.

The Grand Inn
at the
MOUNTAINTOP

As they got out of their car, the Hoffmans noticed a small cemetery beside the inn.

"That's kind of creepy," said Craig.

The front door of the inn creaked open, and a man stepped outside. He was hunched over, and he **shuffled** more than he walked. The soles of his shoes scraped along the porch's splintered wooden floorboards.

"Speaking of creepy," whispered Craig.

"I am Mr. Underhill, the innkeeper here at the Grand Inn," the man said in a raspy, wheezing voice. His coal-black eyes were sunk deep into his face, set off by his pale white skin.

"Welcome. Come in," he said.

Walking through the doorway, Craig saw the inn's old, dusty lobby. It looked like something out of a horror movie.

"This place looks like it could be haunted," Melanie whispered to Craig.

"As a matter of fact, young lady," said Mr. Underhill, overhearing Melanie's whisper, "many people believe that it is."

Melanie's eyes opened wide. "There's a ghost here?" she asked. "Like, a real ghost?"

"Come on," said Craig. "There's no such thing as ghosts."

"Well, now," Mr. Underhill began, in a cracked voice that made everything he said sound **ominous**. "I've been told that some guests have heard a little girl's voice crying out for help. They believe she haunts the inn."

Dad looked doubtfully at the innkeeper and said, "I don't mean to be rude, Mr. Underhill, but my wife and I study history. We heard that you have a very good library, filled with *real* history, not ghost stories."

"Of course," replied Mr. Underhill, eyeing the family, his neck twisted, his sunken eyes glistening like black marbles. "The inn's library is open to all guests. And, as it turns out, you are our only guests at the moment."

As their parents finished checking in, Melanie grabbed her brother by the arm and pulled him aside.

"What if *we* searched for the ghost?" she asked. "Then maybe this might not be the worst weekend ever."

"I guess," moaned Craig. "At least it'll be something to do."

Melanie smiled. "Cool! We're going to find a ghost!"

CHAPTER 2

Ghost Hunting

That evening, as their parents settled into the inn's library to research the area's history, Craig and Melanie started their search for the ghost at the Grand Inn.

They made their way up the winding staircase. It creaked and moaned with every step. Reaching the second floor, the young ghost hunters walked slowly down a dimly lit hallway.

"Maybe this guy should pay his electric bills," **quipped** Craig.

"I came prepared," said Melanie, pulling a small flashlight from her pocket and flipping it on. Its narrow beam revealed a series of oil paintings hanging on the wall—dusty portraits of people long dead, their painted eyes staring out from cracked canvases.

"These are some creepy-looking dudes," said Craig.

Melanie grabbed her brother's arm. "Craig," she whispered excitedly, focusing her flashlight's beam on a large portrait of an old man in the center of the wall. "The eyes on that one. They moved! As soon as I put my light there, they looked right at me."

Melanie aimed her flashlight at the portrait again. The man's eyes remained staring straight ahead.

"They're not looking at us," Craig **scoffed**. "Next you'll be saying that the man in the painting can jump out of the picture."

The kids continued down the hall, guided by Melanie's flashlight. They had taken only three more steps when they heard a loud noise.

CRRR-RASH!

Spinning around, they saw that the painting they had just been looking at had fallen from the wall and smashed to the ground.

"Well, how did that happen?" asked Melanie, her voice trembling.

"Old walls. A flimsy picture hook. It could be anything," replied Craig.

The kids headed back down the hall. Rounding a corner, Melanie felt a chill rush through her body.

"I feel her!" she said, shivering. "I feel the ghost's cold spirit!" She closed her eyes and called out to the ghost, "I'm looking for you. Help me find you."

Craig walked quickly to the end of the hall. "No, *I'll* help you," he said, reaching up and closing an open window. "Has the ghost left?"

Melanie felt the cold chill stop. She sighed in disappointment. "I thought I felt the ghost."

"Just because you want to believe that this place is haunted doesn't mean that it *is*," said Craig.

Melanie said nothing as she walked back to the staircase and up to the next floor.

A door at the end of a long hall swung open just slightly when they reached the next floor. Melanie froze in her tracks.

"Mr. Underhill said we were the only guests," she whispered nervously. "So who's opening that door?"

The door swung back, closing on its own.

Craig led the way down the hall. He and Melanie tiptoed toward the door. They felt the floorboards bend and creak under their steps. They opened the door slowly and peered into a dark closet that smelled **musty**.

Melanie shone her flashlight into the closet. Two glowing eyes stared back at them.

"The ghost!" shouted Melanie.

Re-owwwww!

A big black cat jumped from the top shelf, landed at Melanie's feet, and then raced out of the closet.

"There's your ghost," said Craig.

Melanie nodded, disappointed again—and a bit shaken—but still determined to find the ghost.

Craig and Melanie continued up to the next floor. At each bend in the stairs, the flashlight shone on scary carvings sitting on the stair railing.

"Ooh, creepy," Craig said in a dramatic voice, nudging Melanie with his elbow, as the flashlight hit a particularly **grotesque** carving.

At the top of the stairs, they turned down a hallway.

THUNK, THUNK, THUNK.

They suddenly heard loud footsteps coming toward them. Melanie's heart started beating rapidly. Was she finally about to come face-to-face with the ghost?

CHAPTER 3

Clues from the Past

A large figure stepped out from the shadows. Craig and Melanie quickly backed away.

"Hello—I'm Mrs. Underhill," said the tall woman before them. She towered over the two children, her face deeply wrinkled, her thin gray hair clipped atop her large head. "I'm the housekeeper here at the inn. I know you've met my husband already. May I help you with something?"

Craig nervously spoke up. "My sister thinks that she can find the ghost that haunts this place."

Mrs. Underhill's eyes opened wide. "Oh, I don't believe those old ghost stories," she said. "There is, however, an **unsolved** mystery in this house. Many, many years ago, the inn's cook lived here with her two children. When her son was twelve and her daughter was eleven, the girl disappeared. She was never found. The police believe that she died and that her bones may be somewhere in this house. The rest of the girl's family is buried in our cemetery. If the police found the body, then she could finally join her family there."

"Now, *that's* a mystery I'd like to solve," said Craig.

"I am certain that the clues leading to the missing girl are hidden somewhere in this house," said Mrs. Underhill. "But no one has ever been able to uncover them."

Then, without another word, she turned and slipped back into the shadows.

The following morning, the Hoffman family gathered for breakfast in the inn's dining room.

"Your mother and I are enjoying digging through the historical records in the library here," said Dad between bites of toast. "The inn has an amazing collection of local history. How about you kids? What have you been up to?"

"We've been doing some digging ourselves," said Melanie.

"Yeah, digging for a ghost," added Craig, rolling his eyes.

"But we also discovered that there is a real mystery in this place," Melanie said quickly, knowing that her parents did not believe in ghosts. "A girl disappeared here a long time ago, and she was never found."

"Sounds awful," said Mom.

"Sounds awesome!" said Craig, much more interested in this adventure now that the hunt was for a skeleton.

"What have you learned so far?" asked Dad.

"Right now we're looking for clues," said Melanie.

"Well, maybe we can help," said Dad. "We'll keep our eyes open as we do our research."

"Thanks, Dad!" said Melanie, tossing her napkin on the table and getting up. "Come on Craig, we've covered most of the floors, but we haven't been down to the cellar yet."

"Sure," said Craig through a mouthful of toast. "Whatever you say, Sherlock."

The heavy wooden cellar door opened with a loud squeak. Melanie reached for the light switch on the wall and flipped it up.

Nothing happened.

She flipped it down and then up again. Still nothing but darkness.

Melanie switched on her flashlight and led the way down the stairs. With each step they took, Melanie and Craig **plunged** deeper into darkness, guided only by the narrow beam of the flashlight.

At the bottom of the stairs, Craig tried to stay close to his sister. His sneakers squished on the cellar's wet dirt floor.

"Gross!" he said.

"Shh!" warned Melanie. "I don't think Mr. Underhill would like us looking around down here."

"I don't think *I* like us looking around down here," said Craig.

Melanie swept her flashlight's beam around the cellar. It revealed an old sink, rusty bed frames, and crooked shelves filled with jars of something goopy looking.

Whirr! Whirr! Whirr!

Melanie and Craig jumped at the sudden noise. Melanie whipped her flashlight toward the noise and **illuminated** the inn's furnace as it rumbled and hissed into action.

Scrape, scrape, scrape. Tap, tap, tap.

"What's that noise?" Craig asked.

The noise got closer.

SCRAPE, SCRAPE, SCRAPE. TAP, TAP, TAP.

It sounded like lots of feet rushing near them.

"There's someone down here!" Melanie whispered.

In the narrow pool of light, they saw . . . a line of tiny mice racing along the floor near the wall.

"Ewww!" Melanie shrieked.

"Aaah!" Craig shouted.

The kids backed away from the mice—and bumped right into someone behind them.

"AAAIIIEEE!" they both screamed, spinning around.

Melanie lifted her flashlight. It shone into a pair of coal-black eyes.

CHAPTER 4

A Big Discovery

"Mr. Underhill!" Melanie gasped. "What are you doing down here?"

"Getting the lights in the cellar back on," Mr. Underhill replied. "But I might ask you two the same question."

"We're trying to find clues to solve the mystery of the missing girl," Craig said.

Mr. Underhill raised his eyebrows. "I don't think you'll find anything down here. We searched the cellar already."

"You mean you and Mrs. Underhill?" asked Melanie

"Um … why, yes, of course," Mr. Underhill replied quickly. Flipping on his own flashlight, he screwed a new **fuse** into the fusebox. The lights in the cellar popped on. "Now I think it would be best for us all to go back upstairs."

Mr. Underhill led the way. As Craig and Melanie **emerged** from the cellar, their father met them.

"Oh, there you are," said Dad. "I wanted to show you what we found."

He led the kids into the library, where Mom was reading through a series of newspaper clippings about the missing girl.

"'According to the police, the girl and her brother were playing hide-and-seek when she disappeared,'" Mom read aloud. "'The police searched the whole house but never found her.'"

Melanie looked around the room. "This is one place we haven't searched for clues yet," she said.

The kids scanned the library's lower bookshelves, hoping to find something that would help them unravel the mystery. Their parents searched the higher shelves.

Melanie noticed a beautiful oak cabinet across the room. She opened the cabinet's doors, but it was empty. Then she shone her trusty flashlight underneath it—and something caught her eye.

"I think I found something," she said.

Melanie got down on the floor and stretched her arm to reach the object. It was a **tattered** book.

"This must have been under there for a long time," she said, wiping a thick layer of dust off the cover.

Melanie eagerly opened the book and started reading out loud:

> While strolling around this beautiful old inn,
> I happened to go up to the top floor. It was
> decorated with very pretty tiles. I thought I heard a
> voice—a *faint* cry that sounded like a little girl, saying,
> "Let me out . . ." It must have been my imagination.

"Let me see," Craig said, grabbing the book from his sister and reading aloud.

> Our son swears he heard a little girl's voice
> calling out to him while he was on the top floor. The
> voice said, "Let me out!" He thinks it was a ghost.

"It's a book where guests can write about their stay at the inn," Mom said.

"A book that no one has written in for years," said Dad.

"Yeah, and we found it," said Melanie. "Come on, Craig— let's go find a ghost!"

CHAPTER 5

Secrets Revealed

Craig and Melanie raced up to the top floor of the inn. The hallway was decorated with tiles, just as the guest book had said.

"Look," Melanie said. "All these tiles are neatly lined up."

"Not all," said Craig, pointing to one that was out of line with the others.

Craig twisted the crooked tile to line it up. It moved a bit to the right.

SCRAAAPE! A section of the wall swung inward on rusted **hinges**, revealing a dark passageway behind it.

"We found a secret passageway!" Melanie said.

"No, *we* didn't—*I* did," said Craig, "and I'm going in first!"

"But I'm the one who believes there's a ghost," Melanie argued, shoving her way past her brother and heading into the mysterious passageway. The door swung shut behind her.

Alone in the dark, Melanie reached for her flashlight. She shone the light on the knob and tried to open the door. It wouldn't **budge**.

"Let me out," said a soft voice behind her. She felt a cold hand on her shoulder.

"Craig?" Melanie asked as she spun around and saw . . . a ghostly young girl holding a **flickering** candle.

"Wh-wh-who are you?" Melanie gasped.

"I'm Grace. My mother was the cook at the inn," the girl said.

"One day, my brother and I were playing hide-and-seek. This was such a good hiding place, but I tripped in the dark and hit my head on the hard floor. No one ever found me . . . until now."

The ghost, Melanie thought. *I found her!*

The light from the girl's candle cast a glow on a small skeleton lying on the floor behind her.

"Please take my bones from this place and bury them with my family in the cemetery. Then, at last, I can finally be at rest," Grace said.

While Melanie was trapped in the passageway, Craig ran downstairs to get his parents and Mr. and Mrs. Underhill. The five of them hurried back upstairs and worked to force the passageway door open.

"What happened, Melanie?" Craig asked.

"Are you okay?" Mom and Dad said together.

"A secret passageway!" Mr. and Mrs. Underhill both exclaimed.

"The ghost! The girl! The skeleton! I found her!" Melanie said excitedly. But the ghost had disappeared.

"I'll call the police," Mr. Underhill said.

When the police arrived, they asked Melanie and Craig some questions and **investigated** the secret passageway. Melanie asked what would happen next, and a police officer said that once their report was finished, the girl's **remains** could be placed in the cemetery with her family's.

On his way out, the officer said to Mr. Underhill, "How ya doing, Captain?"

"Captain?" asked Craig.

"Yes, I'm a retired police officer," Mr. Underhill explained. "This girl's disappearance was my case—a case I couldn't solve. I bought the inn hoping to find the girl's remains. I hoped that a ghost story might encourage guests to search the inn and solve the real mystery. And it did! You have brought me great peace of mind."

"So there never really was a ghost," said Craig.

"Oh yes, there was!" insisted Melanie.

At the end of their weekend, as the sun began to set, the family got in their car and drove away from the inn. When Melanie glanced back, she saw Grace's faint figure in the driveway, holding a lit candle. The candle flickered and then suddenly went out. Melanie remembered something that the ghostly girl had said to her: *Every time a candle flickers out on its own, that means a ghost can finally be at rest.*

Then, the ghost suddenly disappeared. And the inn disappeared into the dark night.

The Ghost at the Grand Inn

1. Melanie and Craig think the Grand Inn looks boring at first. Do their feelings change when they learn about the ghost? How?

2. Who is more excited about hunting for the ghost, Melanie or Craig? Use examples from the story and the illustrations to explain your answer.

3. What is this object, and how does it help Melanie and Craig solve the mystery?

4. Who is this character (right), and what does she want?

5. If you visited a haunted inn, would you look for ghosts? Explain why you would or wouldn't go on a ghost hunt.

GLOSSARY

budge (BUHJ) to move or change position

emerged (i-MURJD) came out from somewhere hidden

faint (FAYNT) not clear or strong; hard to see

flickering (FLIK-uhr-ing) shining unsteadily

fuse (FYOOZ) a safety device in electrical equipment that shuts off the power if something goes wrong

grotesque (groh-TESK) ugly, in a strange or creepy way

hinges (HINJ-ez) metal joints on which a door swings open and closed

historic (hiss-TOR-ik) dating from the past, or important in history

illuminated (i-LOO-muh-*nayt*-id) lit something up

investigated (in-VES-ti-gayt-id) gathered information about something

musty (MUHSS-tee) smelling of wetness or decay

ominous (OM-uh-nuhss) giving the feeling that something bad is going to happen

plunged (PLUHNJD) entered suddenly or fell quickly

quipped (KWIPT) said something clever and funny

remains (ri-MAYNZ) what is left of a body after death

sagged (SAYGD) drooped

scoffed (SKAWFD) made fun of something

shuffled (SHUH-fuhld) walked slowly, sliding the feet without lifting them

tattered (TAT-urd) old and torn

unsolved (uhn-SOHLVD) not having an answer or explanation

ABOUT THE AUTHOR

Michael Teitelbaum is the author of more than 150 children's books, including young adult and middle-grade novels, tie-in novelizations, and picture books. His most recent books are *The Very Hungry Zombie: A Parody* and its sequel *The Very Thirsty Vampire: A Parody*, both created with illustrator Jon Apple. Michael and his wife, Sheleigah, live with two talkative cats in a farmhouse (as yet unhaunted) in upstate New York.

ABOUT THE ILLUSTRATOR

Anthony Resto graduated from the American Academy of Art with a BFA in Watercolor. He has been illustrating children's books, novellas, and comics for six years, and is currently writing his own children's book. His most recent illustrated books include *Happyland: A Tale in Two Parts* and *Oracle of the Flying Badger*. You can find his other illustrated books and fine art works at Anthonyresto.com. In his free time he enjoys restoring his vintage RV, and preparing for the zombie apocalypse.